WE COULD BE LIKE THAT COUPLE...

WE COULD BE LIKE THAT COUPLE...

STORIES
SARAH STEINBERG

SEROTONIN | WAYSIDE

INSOMNIAC PRESS

Copyright © 2008 Sarah Steinberg

All rights reserved. No part of this publication may be reproduced, stored in a retrieval system or transmitted, in any form or by any means, without the prior written permission of the publisher or, in case of photocopying or other reprographic copying, a license from Access Copyright, 1 Yonge Street, Suite 1900, Toronto, Ontario, Canada, M5E 1E5.

Edited by Jon Paul Fiorentino

Library and Archives Canada Cataloguing in Publication

Steinberg, Sarah, 1979-
 We could be like that couple / Sarah Steinberg.

Short stories.
ISBN 978-1-897178-58-4

 I. Title.
PS8637.T437W4 2008   C813'.6   C2008-901457-X

The publisher gratefully acknowledges the support of the Canada Council, the Ontario Arts Council and the Department of Canadian Heritage through the Book Publishing Industry Development Program.

Printed and bound in Canada

Insomniac Press, 192 Spadina Avenue, Suite 403
Toronto, Ontario, Canada, M5T 2C2
www.insomniacpress.com

For my mother, one tough cookie.

CONTENTS

We Could Be Like That Couple From That Movie That Was Playing Sometime   1

You Think It's Like This But Really It's Like This   25

The Most Part Of You   49

It's Fine!   75

At Last At Sea   91

Real Peoples   111

WE COULD BE LIKE THAT
COUPLE FROM THAT MOVIE
THAT WAS PLAYING SOMETIME

2   WE COULD BE LIKE THAT COUPLE...

DO YOU KNOW HOW IT FEELS when you need a certain taste in your mouth and instead you have, like, the opposite of that flavour in your mouth and all you want, in that instant, is whatever it is that's going to satisfy that craving? Well, I do. And I also know how it feels when you finally get it. All your taste buds dance and pirouette and leap and jump in ecstasy and your mouth thanks you and screams and moans and oohs and aahs and applauds. Well, that's how I feel about salt. And Jessie.

*

I know Jessie from my ballet class. We've been dancing together for less than a year now, since I was held back again. At sixteen, I should be in Donita's intermediate class, but I haven't been improving much, and they've kept me with Ross for the past two years. My mother teaches the advanced class, and she'd been hoping I would eventually end up with her, but it doesn't look like that's going to happen. At sixteen, you pretty much know if you're good enough, or thin enough, to ever be a dancer. I just turned sixteen, but I think everyone already knows. I see myself in the mirror and I know that the roundness in my stomach, shoulders, and breasts isn't going to get me very far. I see the way my teeth stick out in the front. And my hair looks so coarse and dirty next to Jessie's perfectly smooth, dark bun. But I won't even compare myself to her, because she's another story altogether. Jessie's fifteen, and I think everybody knows that she could really make it. She started pretty late, I think only two years ago, but she's just whizzing past everyone else. She's just so perfect for it—she has this perfect tiny little face with perfectly tiny little features, and she has this super-long, thin body. Everything on her is thin and long, even her eyelashes. She could probably be a movie star. In fact, I think I've seen a movie where the lead actress looks kind of like her. Only Jessie's more beautiful.

My mom comes in and watches over some of the junior lessons, and Jessie became her favourite pretty fast. After only a couple of months in Ross's class, my mom was already coming in and talking to Jessie about taking a couple of extra classes with Donita—so now she's doing both. Jessie was first invited over to dinner then too, and you should have seen how my mother went out of her way. She made the kind of meal she used to try to get me to eat; low in carbs, lots of greens, hardly any salt. The entire time Jessie was over at our place, my mother just kept talking about how to eat properly if you want to be a dancer. And Jessie was hanging on her every word. She must really want to make it. Me, on the other hand, I had to sneak into my bedroom, lock the door, and pull out my private stash of peanuts and beef jerky. I guess I don't want it as bad as Jessie or my mom. You'd think I'd be bitter, but I'm not. I want other things just as bad. So I understand.

*

My mother was a dancer in the Jeffery Tealer Modern Dance Company. She danced Adele in one of his famous requiems. Adele was the lead female. In the dance, Adele was this cat-like, flirtatious, young woman that all of the men wanted, except of course, for the man that *she* wanted. Isn't that just always the way? Well, not really in her case, because in real life, the Adele and Christophe characters were totally in love, and they married and had me. Before they knew I was going to be a girl, they decided they'd name me after their characters. Either Adele Christophe, or Christophe Adele. But I'm glad I'm a girl, because I don't like my middle name very much. Anyway, in my favourite part of the dance, Adele, my mother, was spinning from one end of the stage to the other, and all the men in the company were standing in a semicircle. She stopped at each man, and they leaned in heavily towards her, but she would just spin away while each of them plunged to the floor, dying of grief and unrequited love for Adele. But then she came around to my father, and she tried to spin into his arms, but he moved back just at the last moment, and she was just left there, spinning all on her own. It was so sad. But not in real life.

*

Well, maybe it was kind of sad in real life. My father died when I was nine years old. My mother had to leave the company when she found out she was pregnant with me, but my father had stayed on. I was only six years old when they first figured out that it wasn't just a cold, but it wasn't until after he died that my mother found out about the really horrible stuff. Oh, she's never forgiven him. It turns out that he had begun an affair with Jeffery Tealer during the year that my mother was pregnant with me. I can't imagine how he managed to keep it from her. But I do remember when she found out, although I don't remember too much from the funeral. I remember Jeffery made a speech, and I remember standing behind my mother, clinging to the back of her coat. It was winter, and Jeffrey's words came out in little white puffs. Everybody wore black, like in the movies. Some of the women and men held tissues up to their eyes, but mostly everybody just stood there, staring down at the ground or at the coffin. My mother didn't want me to look at the body; she said she didn't want me to remember my father like that, but I went up anyway. My father was so beautiful. His face was so relaxed, and calm. It looks like a photograph in my memory now.

*

Jeffery hosted the wake. He wore a suit for the occasion. I'd never seen him in one before, and I'd never imagined he could wear anything besides his brown cardigans and slacks. He looked like Mister Rogers to me. He was so tall and thin, and he even had the same thick-rimmed glasses. I guess I expected him to live in the same kind of place, full of little knick-knacks, and soft pastel colours, with maybe a toy train in the middle of the room. But he didn't. In fact, his place was like the opposite of Mister Rogers's house. It was huge, with these great big paintings on the wall that looked like someone had just emptied a paint can onto them, and marble floors that were cold on your bum if you sat down on them. But I liked his place anyway and especially the big, shiny, black piano in the middle of the room, which I sat under that day, licking my finger and sticking it into a salt shaker and then sucking—and hoping no one would notice.

There were a bunch of adults in the room; they were all drinking wine and talking quietly to each other, and nobody noticed me sitting under there. I must have been the only kid there. Then I remember my mother coming out of another room, crying, with Jeffery behind her. She grabbed me from underneath the piano and pulled me out of the room with both of our coats in her hands. I turned around and looked at Jeffery. He waved at me and he said, "Goodbye, Adele," and I noticed that everyone in the room had turned around and was looking at us. My mother held my hand tight as we walked to the car and I remember that she wouldn't stop to let me put my coat on, even though it was freezing outside and I could feel the wind coming into my dress from underneath.

*

We never saw Jeffery again, which I thought was horrible at the time. He was always so nice to me. When we would go to visit my father at the studio, Jeffery used to pick me up and twirl me around and promise that one day he would make a dance for me. He used to sing me the song from the Sara Lee cake commercial, putting my name in the song instead. "Everybody doesn't like something, but nobody doesn't like Adele Christophe..." When he would put me down I would do a little dance for them or show them what I had learned at ballet, and they would stand there and watch me and then they would all three of them laugh and applaud, and Jeffery told me that one day I would be a beautiful dancer, just like my mother and father.

*

I know it sounds silly, but in spite of what happened, I still know my father really loved my mother. I don't remember seeing them together very often but I've seen lots of photographs. In a lot of them, my mom and dad are facing the camera, sometimes in costume and with makeup caked onto their faces, and my dad'll have his arm around my mom. She'll be smiling away at the camera and he'll be looking straight at it, although in a lot of them he looks kind of tired, probably from the shows they did. In my favourite one, she's wearing this long, elegant white dress and holding a glass of white wine and laughing. My father is behind her, sitting in a chair with a cigar in his hands, staring at her from across the room. Of course, in the picture, you can also see Jeffery standing next to my father's chair, staring at him. This is what I've always thought about the affair he had: Jeffery was in love with him so deeply that he made my father be with him, or else he would throw him out of the company. That's just the kind of man my father was. Everyone was in love with him.

*

Anyway, after all that, we moved—and that's when my mother took her job as artistic director and assistant head of the Avenue Road Dance School for Girls. I think she used to be pretty disappointed in me for not excelling at what she does best, but Jessie is starting to change all that for me, so I'm happy. I know that my mom expected me to be a dancer, but I think she figured out a long time ago that it wasn't going to happen. I haven't even managed to master my posture yet. And like she's always told me, not only am I at risk for a heart attack based on all the salty foods I eat, but I will, and do, perpetually retain my water. It's just too bad that I don't look more like Jessie with her thin arms and long legs, because maybe then I wouldn't be so clumsy when I move. But it doesn't matter. It's like all the grace and elegance that I was expected to have was transferred over to Jessie. Which means that she gets to come over for dinner all the time. Which is great. Lately, my mom hasn't even been searching around in my room for my private stashes, which I've learned to hide in different places every week or so. And when she comes into our dance classes, I don't feel the heat of her shame radiating in my direction anymore. Now it's all cool excitement, directed right at Jessie.

*

Everything would be pretty good, except I don't know what to do about Jessie. She was over at our place this weekend, and when my mom went back to the studio I asked her if she'd like to stay and watch a movie. I offered her the choice of any of the movies we've got, even though

I've seen them all a million times. She couldn't choose between *Gone with the Wind* and *Singin' in the Rain*, but she finally decided on *Gone with the Wind*, though I didn't think she would. I sat down on the couch, cross-legged like her, and our knees were touching. When I told her that I thought she was prettier than Scarlett O'Hara, she smiled at me and told me that I was, too. Now, I know I'm not really—but beauty is in the eye of the beholder, I guess. Then, when we got to the part where Scarlett and Rhett kiss for the first time, I turned around and watched Jessie's face. Oh, she looked so excited! And that's when it happened to me. It was exactly like when I have an unexpected salt craving. It just hit me right then and there—my mouth got all watery for a minute and then it dried up and then I knew that if I didn't give her a kiss, I would choke. I thought I'd better start slow, so as soon as Rhett and Scarlett finished their kiss I leaned over and gave her a little one on the cheek. She didn't even see it coming, she was so into the movie. I leaned back after I did it and waited. She didn't do much. She kinda looked over at me quick and cocked her head to one side, and then I guess she heard Scarlett say a line or something, because she turned around and went right back to watching the screen.

*

When the movie was over, Jessie was crying. She thought it was so sad, and I guess it is—but I'm pretty much immune to it, after like, the hundredth time. As the tape rewound, she was sitting there, staring at the blank screen, shaking her head and saying, "It's just so sad. It's just so sad." I put my arm around her and started rubbing her back. I said, "It's okay, Jessie. It'll be okay. I think there's a sequel." And then I gave her a hug. It was a perfect movie moment.

*

I have this great memory. It was the first time I ever went to a film festival, and my father and Jeffery took me. I remember being disappointed because there wasn't any popcorn, but then we went into this huge theatre and I sat in between Jeffery and my dad. There were these enormous, heavy looking, red velvet curtains that parted right before the movie began. It was very exciting. And the movie was great too. It was about this woman, and she was living in France, and she was married to a rich, but mean, man. Or maybe they were living in New York. Anyway, the woman, she was super, but very sad, until she met her husband's sister. Or maybe it was her husband's niece. So anyway, the two women fell in love with each other and they spent all their time together. But actually, I'm not sure. Maybe they didn't fall in love. Maybe it was that the wife fell in love with the sister, or the niece, but she didn't fall in love back. In the end, I think I remember that the woman packed her bags and got on a bus. The last scene had her looking out the window of the bus on the highway, and everything was going by so fast, it looked like little dabs of paint colour. But see, I'm not sure anymore. It was a long time ago.

*

Last night, as I was getting in from class, the telephone was ringing. I ran to pick it up, but I tripped over my scarf and missed it. The answering machine caught it. I picked the message up, hoping that it would be Jessie, but it wasn't. It was a man I'd never heard of before, who called himself Jeffrey's "partner." Now, I didn't know that Jeffery had a business partner, but I guess he is getting older now, and maybe he needs someone to take care of the business end of his affairs. I didn't know that my mom was in touch with Jeffery at all—or anyone who even knew him, but I was sure glad to hear it. It means that I'll finally get to see him again. In any case, this man, he didn't say much in the message, except that it was urgent and that he had found my mother's number at the studio and that he would try to reach her there. I felt pretty pleased about that. I was looking forward to telling my mom about the message, but I fell asleep on the couch watching a made-for-TV version of *A Streetcar Named Desire*, with Melanie Griffith as Blanche. By the time my mom got in it was late, and I woke up when I heard her close the front door behind her. She didn't look in on me in the living room, even though the TV was still on. I sat up on the couch and listened to the sound of her feet on the hardwood floor as she walked straight through the kitchen and down the hall to her bedroom. I could hear that something was wrong with her just by the way she was walking; it just wasn't as soft and rhythmic as usual. I heard her close the door to her bedroom, and that's when I got up and walked to her room. I knocked on the door, but she didn't answer me. I just wanted to tell her about the message on the answering machine, so I opened the door and walked in. She hadn't turned on any of the lights and she was already in bed, lying on top of the covers. I could see that she hadn't even changed into her nightdress. I started to tell her about the message; I got halfway through the sentence, but she interrupted me. "Adele," she said, "go to bed." Her voice sounded sharp and pretty serious. So I turned around and closed her door and got ready for bed. But it didn't change my mood. We're going to talk to Jeffery soon. Things with Jessie are going well. And I haven't been having too many cravings lately. Things are looking good.

*

Every year in spring, my mother puts together a big show that the whole school performs in. A few weeks ago she told me that she's been thinking about choreographing a ballet of the dance that she and my father did in Jeffrey's company. The one that I'm named for. Of course I won't get to be Adele; that would be pretty much impossible and everybody knows that Jessie will get it. But I can dance Christophe, and I know, I just *know* that my mother will give it to me if I promise to stay off the salty foods, and take really good care of my body. I will promise to lose ten pounds for the part. I will promise to rehearse every day, and I will promise to get it right.

*

On the night of the performance, I will wear a beautiful costume. My makeup will be just right. I will be backstage with all of the other girls for most of the performance, being hushed by my mother and trying to sneak peeks into the audience. Then, towards the middle of the show, there will be my first meeting with Adele— our pas de deux—I'll come out onto the stage and take my position. I'll keep my head down. I won't look up when Jessie, I mean Adele, comes onto the stage. I'll stare directly at the audience, like we rehearsed. When Adele makes her circle around me, I will not look up at her. When she tries to persuade me to look into her eyes, I will not. And then, when she finally leaves me alone, I will not change the expression on my face. It will be cold and distant, just like my father when he was me.

*

Then the intermission will come and I'll be thirsty and hungry and tired, but I won't run to my bag and get my crackers. I'll only drink just a little bit of water and imagine all of the people who've come to see us. All the parents and friends and brothers and sisters and aunts and uncles who will be standing in the front hall, sipping on the free coffee and tea, and talking about how terrific the show is. My mother will give us dancers a little speech. She'll tell us how wonderful we've all been, that the show is an absolute success, that everybody in the audience is smiling, they all love it. She'll look at me when she says this, and so will Jessie, who will be so proud of me for being her magnificent Christophe, her one true love.

*

And then the second act will come. Every one of us girls will be hot and sweaty from the lights but we'll also be so excited. The music will come back on, Mozart's *Requiem*, and Adele will perform her first solo. Any shuffling and settling back in to the seats from the audience will stop and they'll all be extra quiet—maybe somebody will sneeze but for the most part, it will all be wowed, expectant faces—all staring at this elegant, perfect beauty in front of them. As for me, I will be waiting for my next scene, when all of the dancers playing men file onto the stage and form a semicircle around Adele.

*

It will be my favourite part of the dance. Adele will be gorgeous. She will move slowly, carefully, towards each man. She will turn towards them, spinning gracefully, lovely. Each man will wait for her, wait until she gets close enough, and then they will lean their bodies in close until she is ready to give herself to them. But she will not. Each man will then fall to the floor, dying, dying, out of grief and unrequited love for Adele. And then she will approach Christophe, the only figure still standing. I will do it all just as I've rehearsed it. I will keep my chin up, away from Adele's heart. I will not watch as Adele does her quiet dance for me, where she shows me, through her opened arms and slow, deliberate movements, how she loves me. And then it will be time for Adele to run across the floor, and then approach me again, this time spinning towards me, keeping her beautiful eyes on me. This is the part where I let her come very close, I let her spin into me—almost—but at the last moment, I turn away, leaving her there, spinning all on her own.

*

But that is not what I do. I cannot do that. Instead, when it comes time for me to cross my arms and turn my back, I open them instead. I open them and I move towards Adele. Nobody expects it, but it looks beautiful. I do not let her fall to the ground, dying out of lack of love. I let her do what she is supposed to do. She dances beautifully. And I do not turn away. I let her fall into my arms.

*

WE COULD BE LIKE THAT COUPLE... 23

YOU THINK IT'S LIKE THIS
BUT REALLY IT'S LIKE this

IN THE MIDDLE OF A DOWNTOWN art gallery, Rhonda had one hand shoved deep inside the mouth of her purse when she made eye contact with her linguistics professor. She found some Kleenex, dabbed her eye with it, and stuffed it back inside.

"Are you okay?" Professor Halle asked as he walked towards her, one hand in the pocket of his chinos and motioning, with his chin, in the direction of her purse. Rhonda had not even had time to think before the words popped out of her mouth.

"It'th okay. I jutht can't control my eye excrethionth."

In bed that night she replayed her response over and over. I just can't control my eye excretions. Thinking about it forced her to get up and eat a whole row of jam cookies, just to get the sour taste of stupidity out of her mouth.

But that was basically it: her eyes had watered. It wasn't like the paintings had moved her. They were stupid, enormous velvet canvases with images she'd seen before: dogs playing cards around a poker table, sad clowns, Elvis with one hand on a microphone, leaning on his hip. Rhonda had stood in the same place for twenty minutes that night, watching Halle not look at her. When Rhonda heard the words come out of her mouth she'd tried to stop them but found that they had already left her. Halle's smile reached around and grabbed his ears, his little perfect ears, and Rhonda was left standing, red faced.

"So what do you think of the show?" he'd said.

"It'th well, I gueth...."

At the beginning, Rhonda thought Professor Halle's kind attitude towards her was due to her lisp. She had imagined he thought of her as some kind of overgrown experiment, a young woman with a child's phonology. But that was before.

*

With her fist squeezed into a ball and shoved as far inside her mouth as it would go, Rhonda repeated the alphabet over and over again, the letters coming out of her in harsh, round grunts. Lying in bed, she found her notebook with her other hand and flipped through her class notes. Aloud, she read the words that Professor Halle had spoken. They were like a private poem, words meant just for her. Rhonda inserted her own slow, deliberate cadence. How can the content of belief enter into the causation or the explanation of behaviour? Rhonda listened for his voice in her own. When she didn't find it, she removed her fist from her mouth, and rolled over onto her stomach.

*

Five days earlier, in the common room, Rhonda had sat with her arms wrapped around her knees, facing her roommate. At first, Rhonda had been intimidated by Elyse: she seemed so poised, so grown-up. But eventually what was happening with Professor Halle had come out, in bits and pieces, and Elyse had taken the case up with sincere interest.

Rhonda was in her pyjamas, a flannel top and bottom set dotted with images of ponies jumping over barrels. She sipped on a can of Diet Coke through a fat green straw that wound and doubled over itself near the top and tugged on a strand of black hair that had come loose from her ponytail. A gaggle of young women could be heard making their way down the hallway, screeching and guffawing together. Rhonda waited until they passed through the common room and got into the elevators before she continued, her voice a theatrical whisper.

"Well, the thituathon might be a little weird, but the truth ith that he hath to realize that if he wanths thingth to be the way that they uthed to, he hath to talk to me. He can't jutht keep ignoring thith thituation."

Across from Rhonda on the other couch, Elyse switched from program to program expertly, almost completely avoiding the commercials. Mostly she divided her attention between *Maury*, in which a middle-aged man was about to reveal to his new wife that he was the fraternal twin of her late husband, and MTV's *MADE*, an episode that Elyse was particularly riveted by, in which a clumsy and overweight high school Senior wanted to become a cheerleader.

"Yeah, that sounds shitty," Elyse said, and then laughed. The wanna-be cheerleader had just fallen over in an attempt to jump and touch her toes, and she was now sprawled out on a blue gym mat, fat tears welling up in her eyes. Her coach, a professional cheerleader from the Arizona Wildcats, stood over the girl's prostrate body and chastised her.

"That's not cheer!" he said, pointing at her.

"Oh my god, what a nerd!" Elyse said.

Rhonda pulled the straw out of her Diet Coke and chewed on it until it flattened, and her teeth marks made a perfectly symmetrical criss-crossed design. Elyse yawned and stretched out on the couch. Back on *Maury*, the audience was cheering as husband and wife embraced.

"I don't care who you are!" the wife said, "as long as you're my husband."

*

Halle's lectures had always been a source of pleasure. On the first day of class, Rhonda had walked into the lecture hall twenty minutes late. With her books in one hand, and her purse and mug of hot chocolate in the other, she stood in the doorway and looked around for an empty seat. As Professor Halle was talking, he walked over to Rhonda with a syllabus in his hand. He handed it to her, and as he did he swept his eyes across her body, from her jelly sandals to her freckled nose, resting there just a split second longer than is customary. From her spot in the fifth row, chewing on the corner of the syllabus, Rhonda had watched Professor Halle's back when he turned to write *C-Command* and *Generative Linguistics* on the board. That, she had thought, is the back of a man.

As the year had gone on, however, Rhonda had begun to notice other things about Professor Halle. Like how he rolled his shirtsleeves up twice before pushing them up over his forearms, like how his jeans were always dark, how he drank large coffees without the lid on, how he had his hair trimmed every two weeks but sometimes three, how his writing on the board was neat, and the letters were always close together. When he wrote the letter *W*, it was a series of sharp, tight lines. No curves. Rhonda liked his handwriting so much that she began to emulate it in the hope that he would notice how similar their handwriting was and take that as a sign of their like minds. She imagined them signing a Christmas card together: how cute that would look!

*

During an overview of Chomsky's Poverty of Stimulus theory, in which Halle explained that grammar could not be learned and must therefore be innate, Rhonda began to realize that while Halle might be explaining a linguistic theory to the class, he was actually telling her, Rhonda, something very different.

At first, it hadn't occurred to her that it was a code, but he kept saying it, over and over again: poverty of stimulus, poverty of stimulus. Halle began drawing circles around the words he'd spelled out on the board.

"So then," Professor Halle said, his back to the class, "you might at first think it's like this," and he drew yet another circle around the word *nurture*. "But really, actually, it's like this," and here he underlined the word *nature* several times and stabbed the chalk against the board. He turned, triumphantly, to face the class. "Nature."

When Rhonda realized what he was really saying, the tips of her fingers began to tingle. Her stomach felt heavy, as if her lunch were sinking into her groin.

*

When *Maury* broke for commercials, an advertisement

for Cialis came on the television. A man and woman were splashing each other with water. Elyse looked over at Rhonda.

"Don't take this the wrong way but what situation are you talking about?" Rhonda stopped chewing on her straw.

"What do you mean, what thituation? Thee thituation. I told you!" She stared hard at Elyse, and her lower lip stuck out in a charming pout. "It'th been nearly a week."

Elyse looked back at the TV. A male announcer with a deep voice was in the process of enumerating the possible side effects of the drug. For a while, neither of the girls said anything.

"…In rare cases Cialis may cause a sudden loss of vision in one or both eyes," the announcer said.

Elyse didn't turn to face Rhonda when she finally responded. "I don't know. I guess you'd better sort it out then." She shrugged. "I don't know."

*

Rhonda went to the gallery that night because she knew he'd be there. She'd seen a flyer for the event on his office door, and he'd made a joke in class that day about art galleries. It was an obvious sign.

She'd spent over an hour getting ready: brushing her hair, finding just the right ensemble, applying makeup and even, for the first time, a pair of false eyelashes she'd picked up after class. She felt they made her eyes look dramatic; sophisticated, even.

The V Gallery was clean and bright and long, with nothing to lean up against or sit on. Rhonda clutched the strap of her vinyl purse with both hands. Clusters of well-dressed men and women stood at a distance from the paintings, holding napkins with cubes of cheese, broken crackers, and soft grapes on them. They were speaking to each other, but Rhonda couldn't make out any words. Their voices were soft and their faces grieved. Rhonda had never been to an art opening but her uncle had died of lung cancer the year before and all this quiet formality, these hushed voices, felt unexpectedly similar. She would have liked to whisper something to Professor Halle, something safe, something that would not betray the sensitivity of their situation, but the only thing she could think to speak of was her uncle.

"So, have you had a chance to listen to that CD I lent you?" Professor Halle asked. He took a sip from his plastic wine goblet.

That CD? That CD he'd lent her? Was he asking for it back? The thing was propped up on her nightstand like a framed photograph! How could he want it back? It wasn't a loaner, it was like a class ring or a football jacket! No, it couldn't be—he didn't really want it back. He probably just wants to make small talk, Rhonda thought, or he's trying to get me back into his office.

Halle had given it to her after mid-terms. She'd studied with a fierceness that went beyond her usual devotion, staying up all night, reading the material over and over again. But Chomsky was tough. She'd read every single sentence carefully, looking up words she didn't understand, but somehow his meaning still eluded her, and she'd found herself reading the same lines twice, sometimes three times, without even noticing.

The mid-term had not gone well. During the first hour, she'd chewed on her pencil and read the questions, jotting down notes whenever she thought something might apply. By the second hour, she'd chewed a hole through the sleeve of a good wool sweater. By the third hour she'd given up, and with her head and arms on the desk, quietly sobbed. Her returned exam, marked with red ink, looked like a tattersall of callow mistakes. At the bottom of the last page, Halle had requested that Rhonda see him in his office.

He'd never spoken to her out loud. Rhonda stood in the hallway outside his office and waited. She could feel the sweat under her arms absorbing into her T-shirt. Would he notice? Her bladder was beginning to swell. The corners of her test papers were tattered and wet.

The inside of his office was tiny. It allowed for his desk and two bookshelves crammed with books, none of which looked readable. Standing by the doorframe, with her books, arms, and test papers crossed against her chest, Rhonda took a quick look around the room. There was the *Abbey Road* poster next to his computer, a Rubik's cube in mid-solution, a stack of papers on a chair squeezed into the corner of the room. Underneath the chair Rhonda noticed a paper shopping bag with the words *Tom's Health Food* printed in blue ink. Where was that store? She would have to look it up.

"Please, have a seat."

Halle was already sitting. He'd taken his sweater off and was wearing a black, V-neck T-shirt. Rhonda sat down and crossed her legs while Halle leafed through some papers. Halle looked up at her and—Oh Elythe! What peirthing brown eyeth! You should thee them!—she suppressed the urge to giggle.

"Hi," she said instead.

Halle nodded, and smiled at her.

"Well look, I'm glad you came to see me today," he said, and abruptly every sound that was not his voice—the conversation of the students in the hall, the whir of the fan on his computer, the buzz of the fluorescent lights above—stopped.

"I geth I did pretty badly on the extham, but I mean, I thort of underthtand the material, it'th jutht, um...."

Rhonda realized that she had no idea what she was saying. Halle's eyes were wide.

"You have a lisp?" he asked, and cocked his head to the side. Rhonda said nothing, because before she could answer, Halle smiled the most handsome smile she had ever, ever seen.

When she left his office that afternoon, a copy of *The Beach Boys in Concert* clutched in her hands, Rhonda knew that something important had happened to them.

*

Rhonda's first sexual encounter with Halle was going to be her first time. She was ready for it, but how would it happen? Would he hold her back after class again? Show up at her dorm and pretend to need something? After weeks of imagined scenarios, Halle still hadn't made a move.

And then it dawned on her: he hadn't just given her that CD because it had her name in it. It was so much more than that. "Help Me, Rhonda" was Halle's way of telling her he was as disoriented by her as she was by him. It all made sense. So she would have to make the first move, and it would definitely have to happen in the classroom: the most obvious place and therefore the most disguised. Later, when she was no longer his student, they would be open about everything. At the end of the semester he would surprise her with roses and chocolate, take her to a restaurant, hold her hand. In the meantime, she would help them both.

*

One quiet winter evening in her dorm room, with Track 13 on repeat, Rhonda pulled out from under the bed a gift her Auntie Cathy had given her before she'd left for college. It was a book called *My Body* and the cover featured a realistic drawing of a woman, one side of her body without any skin, the bones, muscles, and organs visible.

Rhonda had borrowed one of Elyse's tops: a tight, red sequined number, and worn it to class. Halle had pretended not to notice and Rhonda had teased him by calling attention to herself: she did not stop her teeth from chattering in the cold, and she shivered and rubbed the tops of her bare shoulders with her hands. Launching into his lecture, Rhonda noted the way he casually looked over in her direction every so often.

When it was time, Rhonda followed the book's instruction: contract the pubococcygeus muscle, release, contract, release. At first, nothing happened. She closed her eyes. The soothing harmonies of the Beach Boys filtered in from somewhere deep in the background. She lay in her bed. Professor Halle walked into her room in the dormitory and sat next to her on the bed, stroking her hair. There, next to her, he whispered Dr. Zenon Pylyshyn's lecture on cognitive processing, sometimes getting very quiet and bending down very close to her ear. He ran his fingers down the length of her back. He kissed her shoulder blades, the nape of her neck. Then Professor Halle removed his clothes and got into the little bed with Rhonda, and for a time he wrapped his arms around her and did not move at all.

When she opened her eyes, Halle was looking right at her. It had been wonderful.

But that had been nearly two weeks ago, and since then it seemed as though something had changed. Every relationship had its challenges, Rhonda knew it, but how would they get past this?

She stared at Halle. He took another sip of his wine and looked around the gallery, acting as though he was totally comfortable standing there, in the midst of an awkward, and therefore unpleasant, conversation. Rhonda wanted to stamp her foot.

"No, I haven't finished with the CD," she finally said, and clamped down hard on the words. A tiny piece of spittle leapt out of her mouth and landed in Halle's left eye. He flinched and attempted to bring his hand to his eye, but it held his wine goblet and instead he spilled red wine on his shoulder.

"Shit," he said, and tried to look at his shoulder, wincing, the offended eye shut.

There it was! A wink! She wanted to throw her arms around him! But she was wary, as well. Hadn't he gone cold on her after their last encounter?

"Not tonight!" she said, her tone as disdainful as she could force it to sound. He would have to shape up, she thought, shape up or ship out.

"I don't, what—" Halle looked pained. A woman across the gallery glared at Rhonda in a way that made her feel that they were making a scene.

"I thaid not tonight, and I mean it," Rhonda said, exaggerating her lisp. She felt excited. She wished Elyse were there to witness the moment. "If there'th one thing you can count on Buthter, it'th my word. You can believe that," and she pulled the used Kleenex from her purse. "Here," she said, thrusting it in Halle's direction. "I think you might be needing this," she said, reminding herself of her mother, and feeling suddenly very, very adult.

*

THE MOST PART of YOU

"NOW, YOU JUST PLACE YOUR feet up there," the nurse said, pointing at the stirrups at the end of the gurney, "and the doctor will be here in a moment," so Deanna placed her feet up there in the stirrups, and that made her think of horses.

When the doctor came, a Dr. Bottemer, a name that Deanna thought apt, she smiled—though much too perfunctorily, Deanna felt—and introduced herself, and Deanna considered reaching out her hand, but didn't, and instead laid there like a clam.

"Okay. We're going to get started," the doctor said, reaching for a speculum. The nurse, a grey haired woman in her sixties, turned her attention to a small television screen positioned a few feet from the bed.

"This is so that we can see exactly what's happening up there," Dr. Bottemer said, and then added, "you don't have to look at it if you don't like."

She wasn't sure if she liked or not, but within a few moments the screen was lit up with the fleshy colours of her cervix, or what she was told was her cervix. Certainly it was her body though, and this surprised her, to be in two places at once like that, on the bed and also pinkly on the screen.

"My cervix is a star," Deanna said, to no one in particular, and no one responded.

"Most women only find this mildly uncomfortable or unpleasant, but you let me know if you're in pain."

Deanna nodded and closed her eyes. Within seconds she felt herself in intense pain. Sharp, pinching, cramping.

"Are you in pain?" Dr. Bottemer asked.

Deanna did not answer, but the nurse, who was looming over her and watching both Deanna and her cervix, and whom she had been obliged to ask, when filling out the forms at the front desk, if number of pregnancies included abortions too, said, rather protectively, "I think it is *emotional* pain," and then Deanna squeezed her eyes shut, and even though she hated her, allowed the nurse to pet her forehead and whisper to her until it was over.

When it was over, the nurse flipped the screen off and both women left. Deanna sat up and waited a few minutes before getting dressed. As she pulled on her jeans she imagined her insides as a dark closet. She saw a hand reaching into it, as if searching around for a lost mitt. She couldn't see the hand's owner, but she knew that whoever was looking for the mitt wasn't going to find it. The hand waved around in the closet, grasping at things. A cockroach scurried out.

*

"Is *this*, my dearest daughter, what I paid so many thousands of dollars for you to go to school for? Hmm? An honours degree in history and you're working for minimum wage?" Her mother pronounced each syllable. Min-i-mum, mini-mum, mini-mom.

Deanna's job as a cook in a daycare was supposed to have been temporary, the first summer out of school only. At first she didn't like it: pizzas, spaghetti, peas and corn, fish sticks, mashed potatoes. Burning herself when she dropped the potatoes into the boiling water which caused little blisters on her wrists and cheeks, the sound of screaming children who didn't want to nap, the bright fluorescent lights, the loud primary colours, the finger paintings everywhere, and above all the other two women who worked there. These women! These women wrapped their arms around every, any, all of the kids, talked of nothing else but the kids, all the time, at work, and even, she imagined, at home.

But then something had changed. The gluey smells of the daycare became familiar and then reassuring. On breaks she would leave the building and sneak around back where she could flip through books for toddlers and smoke. Bernard goes to school. Bernard makes a friend. Bernard makes a poop. It was a simple life, she told herself. It was a comfort. And if there is one thing a person needs in this life, Deanna told herself, it is some comfort.

*

When Chad told her it was over the blues records he had left in her apartment had sat untouched for weeks, stacked menacingly against the wall in her bedroom, until one night when she pulled them out and braced herself. But it turned out it was nice to listen to the music. She nodded as she listened, not to the beat but in sympathy. Lying on her bed, eyes closed, she agreed. Yes, yes, I want a little bit of sugar, too.

She felt she understood the music. Better, at least, than she could understand anything else. That was the thing: when Chad left, Deanna suddenly realized that she, unlike everyone else, did not understand a thing. The world looked too strange to her. She heard of street signs in Brooklyn that read: No Honking—$500 Fine, and marvelled over it for days. She remembered a thimble someone had shown her once, from the Rock and Roll Hall of Fame in Ohio—a thimble (!) with the museum's name printed on it in tiny blue letters. She'd heard of a man who had survived being hit by lightning and run over by a train on two separate occasions, about a woman who'd had fifty-seven cosmetic surgeries. Hearing about things like this made her feel both uneasy and excited. Peeling potatoes or dicing peppers, she wondered if the world she remembered from before was the same as the one she was in now. They didn't seem the same. Certainly she remembered herself differently.

*

"He is so cute, oh my god, that Michael," Ingrid said, standing in front of the open fridge. "I swear I could just eat him up!" and then Ingrid made an eating-him-up sound—gobble-gobble—and put her fingers to her mouth, and Rachel, seated at the small table behind her, laughed.

Delicate and small, Ingrid was the kind of beauty that Deanna particularly admired. Her hair looked as if it had never been cut or styled, and yet it fell from her head in perfectly loose ringlets, it actually *cascaded*, and her hands were thin and elegant—her fingers, in particular, were long and perfectly formed. Plus, Ingrid was nice. There was no other word that so rightly described her. She seemed to have absolutely no sense of her beauty, of the power of her beauty, and if Deanna felt slightly uncomfortable around her it was because of this, because she had never met anyone who seemed so totally insensible of their own capacity to silence a room, someone so thoroughly well-intentioned.

"I think we should put his painting here," Rachel said, waving a piece of white construction paper with several misshapen circles on it. "Is that okay with you if we put this up on your fridge?" she said to Deanna, walking over towards the oversized refrigerator. She patted Ingrid on the back and Ingrid moved so that Rachel could bend down and move the other paintings aside. Michael was new to the daycare. He was a cherubic and precocious three year old. He said "wookie" instead of cookie, something that Deanna had been told on several occasions was, seriously, the most darling thing ever to occur. Ever.

"Sure," Deanna said, trying to sound, if not delighted, than at least not totally apathetic. "Of course."

"It's so bad that you don't get more one-on-one time with the kids, Deanna," Ingrid hummed, making her way back to the little table in the corner of the room. "Don't you think?"

Deanna stood with her back towards the girls, rinsing the dishes before setting them in the washer.

"Um," she said, clearing some phlegm from her throat. "Um, you guys are really great with them."

Ingrid and Rachel both turned to look at her. "Aww," they said in unison.

"That is *so* sweet!" Ingrid said, and rushed over to give Deanna a hug. "I'm gonna go check on them. But you know what? We're going out for dinner on Friday. You should really join us. Huh, Rachel?"

Rachel looked over at Deanna and nodded her head enthusiastically. "Yeah, we're going to Carlos and Pepe's. Come. Best margaritas ever."

"Uh huh," Ingrid said, on her way out of the kitchen. "Rachel just loves them."

*

At home, Deanna checked her messages to find one from the clinic. It was a receptionist, asking her to call back, but she didn't have a pen handy and then, out of habit, she erased the message immediately. But it was okay, she figured. They would call back if it was that important.

Her routine after work was simple. She undressed, turned the television on, and then sat down in front of it. Usually she stayed there all night, sometimes taking the time to cook dinner and sometimes not. A couple of times a week she rolled up some weed she bought from a neighbour, and when she did that she could never concentrate on the television well enough to sit still in front of it, and so she would find herself up and about the apartment, walking around, as if exploring. She would put on one of the records and find herself immersed completely in that deep and straightforward sorrow.

Although she hated that it was his music that moved her, that it was, in a sense, *him* that moved her, she could not keep herself from it, because, simply, it felt good. All over the walls of her apartment there were little penciled indications of the nights she spent like this. In her bedroom, for instance, above her bed, she had written the word "time"; above the record player she had written the words, "dance" and "ha!" and "sugar," and in other places, on other walls, she had written other words and phrases: "bless you," "sweep," "vast," "yes," "bounce." Once, after reading a few pages from a Bruce Lee biography she had plastered the words "walk on" to her window with sticky letters she'd found at the dollar store, but when the L had fallen off she had been forced to rearrange them and had been unable to come with anything besides "wank."

On these nights Deanna felt good: she exalted in the idea of compassion, love, inner peace. She would feel a wave of forgiveness towards Chad, because in those moments she understood that this was life, that people got hurt, that relationships end. But then, when the records were through and it was late, she would lie awake with her eyes shut tight, fighting back a growing anxiety that said you will never, ever make it out of this.

*

Friday morning, Ingrid grabbed Deanna by the wrists. "Please come tonight. We think it would be really fun if you did."

She couldn't imagine herself out with the girls. What would they talk about? It had been so long since she had socialized. She could feel Ingrid's small fingers pressing into the soft side of her wrist.

"Okay, great. I will. Thank you."

"Yes!" Ingrid said, and let go of her grip. She put her hand on Deanna's shoulder. "Awesome. We're going to have fun."

Deanna could hear Rachel reading to the kids as she prepared their lunch. Rachel read to the children in such a slow, deliberate, and condescending voice that it sounded, to Deanna, almost like a joke. When the fish sticks came out of the oven, Deanna placed them on their plastic plates. She pulled the peas out of the microwave and lined them up in a semicircle under the fish sticks. She spread the corn out above the eyes, like funny yellow hair, and then dotted the middle of the fish sticks with daubs of ketchup. When Ingrid saw the plates she laughed.

"A happy face? You are so creative!"

But a few minutes after they had brought them out to the children Deanna heard a commotion. Someone was sobbing, there was banging. Seconds later she could hear more crying. When she came out of the kitchen she saw Michael, his plate turned over, the peas and corn spread out on the floor in front of him. He was alternating between stomping his feet and banging his fist into the fish stick smeared on the table. Several other children were crying, too.

"Wookie! I want wookie!"

Rachel hunched over him, her shoulders up around her ears. She rubbed his back and cooed at him. Ingrid moved around the room, attending to the other children. Deanna stood, motionless, in the doorway.

"Michael, sweetie, please. What's wrong? Don't you like your lunch? Look, it's a happy face!"

"Wookie! Wookie!"

"Deanna?" Rachel looked up to see her leaning against the doorframe. "Would you mind taking Michael into the kitchen and giving him a C-O-O-K-I-E? I don't know what else to do with him."

Deanna nodded and walked over to Michael. Abruptly, she picked him up out of his seat. He let out a shriek but once in the kitchen, an arrowroot cookie shoved at him, he stopped his fuss and set about gnawing on it.

*

She'd meant to call the clinic back. The messages from the receptionist had begun to sound increasingly impatient—she had, by now, left three—but by the time Deanna got home she was sure the offices were closed, and she hardly had enough time to shower and get dressed before meeting the girls downtown anyway.

Ingrid and Rachel were well into their second margarita by the time Deanna got there. They looked different. Rachel had applied bright red lipstick and was wearing large gold hoops in her ears. Her hair was pulled back into a ponytail so tight it looked painful. In fact, she looked, anachronistically and not a little uncomfortably, like the girls Deanna had been scared of in high school. Ingrid wasn't as made up but she had changed her clothes and forgone her usual baggy attire for something much more dramatic. Deanna couldn't see what she was wearing on the bottom, but her top was a purple sequined halter that plunged very low at the chest.

"Yay!" They both yelled when they saw her.

The dining room at Carlos and Pepe's was crowded and buzzing. Loud dance music blared from the speakers. Waiters moved around intently, one hand under the big round trays above their heads. Deanna had to strain to hear the girls, both of whom seemed unfazed by the clamour. Rachel was bopping around in her seat, as if she had to pee.

"That was crazy with Michael today, eh?"

Deanna nodded, and soon a waiter came around with a pitcher of margarita.

"We may as well," Ingrid yelled, above the music.

"It was so weird!" Rachel yelled and then shivered and shook her head in a way that reminded Deanna of a wet dog.

The enchiladas came and the nachos came and another pitcher of margarita came, and everything was very salty, and then another pitcher of margarita came, and Deanna began to feel comfortable. Even the annoying thud of the bass became distracting in a kind of pleasurable, trance-like way. When a neighbouring group of co-eds turned the area around their table into an impromptu dance floor, Deanna turned around to look at them, and the sight of two girls trying to peel another friend off their banquette looked plainly sweet in an inclusive and generous kind of way.

Their waiter came over to the table with three tall shots of tequila. Ingrid thanked him and he turned on his heels and disappeared into the crowd.

"So do you see any cute guys?"

Deanna knew she was supposed to turn around to survey the room, but she didn't want to. Instead she thought of the dimple in Chad's cheek, of how innocent and safe it had made him appear to her. Next to Rachel, Ingrid was poking the ice in her drink with her straw.

"Let's play the game," Ingrid said.

Rachel clapped her hands together.

"Okay Deanna, this is what you do. You choose a guy in the room and then you look at him and you see if he makes eye contact with you. Like, Ingrid will choose a guy for me, and if he looks at me I get a point, and if he keeps staring I get two. Get it?"

"Um," Deanna said.

Ingrid set her drink down and nudged Rachel in the side.

"Okay," she said. "Rach, that guy over there, in the weird, like, leisure suit? See him? With the gold baseball hat to the side a bit? Do him."

"Him? You're so mean!"

"Why? Cuz he's uggers? C'mon!"

Rachel and Ingrid were seated with their backs to the wall and had a view of the room. Deanna turned around to search the boy out. She spotted him sitting with a large group of other boys, looking down at his plate and pushing some food around with his fork. Deanna turned back around and watched as Rachel smoothed the top of her hair and applied some lip gloss. She put her elbows on the table and rested her chin in her hands. Both the girls began staring hard. Within a few seconds they laughed. Rachel looked away, pretending to be distracted by her shoulder, but Ingrid kept staring.

"Yep, you got two points," she said. "Deanna it's your turn. We'll both watch for you."

"Um," Deanna said, searching her mind for the right excuse. "I really can't."

"No!" The girls bleated.

"No, come on, you *have* to, we always play the game!" Rachel told her.

"I just, it's not… I can't." Deanna trailed off and looked at her plate of nachos. The cheese had hardened and had begun to sweat. She stared at the empty shot glass in front of her. She thought of the thimble from the Rock and Roll Hall of Fame. She imagined a police officer in Brooklyn, pulling someone over for honking, the brown of his aviator glasses, his hand on his hip, Chad's hip, the hand in the closet that was her cervix.

"Listen, why not? I know it's ridiculous," Ingrid said. "But it's silly, and it's fun. And you'll laugh."

"I have cancer," Deanna said, and watched as Ingrid's smile disappeared. She thought she could see where the wrinkles and laugh-lines would begin on her face, but she could tell that Ingrid would still be beautiful in twenty years. The music seemed to be getting louder; the pounding of the bass echoed in her ears. She saw that Ingrid and Rachel's mouths were opening and closing, the expressions on their faces shocked and nervous and also, she thought, a little excited. But she didn't care to hear whatever it was they were saying. Instead she thought of hoisting herself up onto a horse in Mexico, Chad's hands at her waist, helping to lift her, the sun that afternoon on his back when he took off his shirt and led the horse by the bit, the beads of sweat that gathered at the bottom of his neck, the cool water at the lake they discovered, lying down on the yellow grass and knowing exactly the moment when they had made their first child, the fight on the plane, the afternoon he killed the cockroach for her, in the kitchen, pounding at it with her broom, and then when it was dead how she yelled at him, Chad, you can't do it like that! If it's female the eggs will go everywhere! They'll spread. They'll get into the sugar and then they'll hatch and then there'll be a million babies everywhere and how will I kill them all on my own?

*

It's fine!

YOUR COLOUR ON THE SCHEDULE will be violet. As you can see, all the other colours have been taken. If someone leaves, you can request that we change your colour. For now though, when you see a box on the schedule coloured in with the violet marker, you can go ahead and write that down in your day planner or whatever you use. I do suggest you use something. A calendar or a day planner. We sell day planners if you're interested. I have one and it works well for me. Once you've been here for three months, you will get a discount on store purchases. Do not run the receipt feed for slips of paper to write on. If you need to take a message or write a note, use these slips of paper here. Don't write personal notes with these slips of paper, these are exclusively for messages and to track special requests. A special request is when someone calls the store and requests a book. Usually we have the book but if we don't, we'll order it if we can. We can't always order a book. Sometimes they're out of print or otherwise unavailable. I'll teach you how to do that but not right now. However, if we do have the book, what you do is retrieve it from the shelf, and then write the name and telephone number of the person who requested it. Then put it under the counter, here. Why don't you try that? Try writing a note as if someone has specially requested this book, *The Yiddish Dog*. I'm going to go place it on the shelf. Stay here. Okay, you saw where I put it, right? Imagine that I've just requested it. What would you do? Yes, that's right. Now write the name and phone number of the person who asked for it. Just make up a name, it doesn't have to be mine. But if you can't think of one, just use mine. You thought of a name. Okay, that's funny, very good. So now, put it there. Good. Now take it out. We don't want it sitting there, because if someone comes in to buy that book, they won't be able to find it behind the counter, right? It's important to listen to instruction here. We have a certain way of doing things.

Have you ever worked in a bookstore before? No, that's right. I remember from your application. That's okay. We'll train you. You'll know what you're doing in a few weeks. We don't expect you to know everything all at once. We thought your application was very clever. That's why we gave you the job. You might have thought it was strange that we didn't interview you? We don't do that here. We use your application instead of an interview. That's how we do things. Is this your bottle of water? I see. No that's fine, you didn't know. We don't put liquids of any kind behind the counter. If you have something to drink, I'll show you, follow me. Have you been given a tour of the store yet? Right, but a *tour by a manager*. Well, these are our bestsellers, fiction. We have two kinds of bestsellers. We have bestsellers as they are ranked in the *New York Times*, and we have the store's bestsellers. They're stacked, as you can see, in two different pyramids. I'll explain about the pyramids later: they're very important. What did we come over here for? Oh right. Underneath these pyramids, in that little cubby, that's where you want to place liquids. If you bring a snack to work, a granola bar or something like that, you can put it in that cubby too. Please make sure snacks are sealed in packages, that's an important detail to remember, and also, don't let the customers see you eat. Feel free to come around to this side of the store and have a drink of water, or sip on your coffee, whatever, at any time. Coffee doesn't really stay hot unless it's in a thermos, but we don't encourage thermoses, so it's best if we just ignore that I said it's okay to drink coffee. Let's just stick to water until further notice? It's fine if the customers see you drinking water, but don't let them see you eat. We think it's unprofessional. We don't want crumbs on the floor either. If you do bring a snack and you put it in the cubby, let me know when you feel like eating it. Usually that's fine, and you can take your snack outside and have it there. We don't have a staff room. That? No, that is only for the managers. Well, it doesn't normally get that cold in this city. If it is unusually cold and you'd like to have a snack, just ask me. I'm not a dictator, I'm not going to be unreasonable. Hang on. We're getting ahead of ourselves. What have we covered so far? Your colour, special requests, liquids and snacks. Have we touched on the pyramids?

As you can see, we have a great many books here, and more come in every day. We don't have a stockroom so we do it all out here. That can be very challenging. So. Take a quick look around. We have regional travel guides, those are over there, we have poetry there, we have literary criticism there, there are travel guides for the rest of the world but those are in Miranda, and we have fiction, history, science, philosophy, and books about pets. We make roughly five sales an hour here, so you should be prepared to deal with that. About a hundred people come through the store on a daily basis. Sometimes more. You're probably wondering how I know that. Well, one of our former managers counted, and also I've counted several times myself. We think it's important to know those kinds of details. You'll have to do quite a bit of memorizing here. Are you good with memorization? Your application said you were. Are you catching all this?

Let's go into Miranda. Miranda is the name we've given to the small room. No, it's not named after *that* Miranda. She is a manager though. But it's purely coincidental, although possibly an omen. Have you been in there yet? So then you know that we carry world travel, cookbooks, paperbacks, business, and children's lit in there. Did you have a look at the way the travel is organized? That's okay; this is difficult. See here? This little insignia on the spine of the book? The spine of the book refers to this, this is what we call the *spine* of the book. And this is the publisher's insignia. We arrange travel by publisher alphabetically, then continent alphabetically, then country within the continent alphabetically. Can you find me a guide to Morocco? I'll give you a hint. It's in Africa. Oh, have you? That's very interesting. Yes, of course. I remember you mentioned that in your application. It was an NGO, right? It must have been difficult for you, being a woman there. You'll have to tell me about that sometime, although you should know that we have a strict policy enforced vis-à-vis the fraternizing of managers and employees. In general, we discourage the sharing of personal information? Uh, you'll have to go a lot faster than that. There you go. Good for you. Can you put it back? No. No. No, stop! No. What did I tell you? Publisher, then continent, then country. Alphabetically. This is a *Lonely Planet* guide. That means it begins with the letter L? Therefore, would it go before or after the *Fodor's*? That is correct. And would it go before or after the *Let's Go* guides? Correct. You're getting the hang of it. It won't take long. Don't worry about it, it's fine.

Have you met Miranda yet? She's very busy with a customer right now, I don't want to interrupt her. She is a manager, as I've mentioned. Scott is a manager, David is a manager, I am a manager, Ryan is a manager, and so is Travis and so is Allen. You will be one of two employees. We like to have at least three managers on duty at all times, and two employees. You will be working with me and Travis and Scott, or myself and Ryan and Miranda. Miranda and I have been here for the greatest length of time. We have been here for six and eight years respectively. Miranda has been here the longest, which is why she is the head manager. I have been here for six years, but I worked in another bookstore before that. As you can probably see, I am responsible for the training of new employees. In the event that I am unable to train you, Miranda will take over that responsibility. Feel free to ask her any questions that you would otherwise ask me. We encourage that. Miranda is very knowledgeable. Very intelligent. I should not mention this but I will: Miranda is a writer. She is currently writing a great American novel. Oftentimes she is not here. You will notice that. That is because she is working on her novel. We are all supportive of that. Miranda is the head manager, so she is able to choose her days on and off. That's a manager's privilege. It would upset the balance here if everyone were able to choose their own schedule. You'll be working six days a week, eight hours a day. I see. Well, your application said that you could work, and I quote, whenever. Six days a week is not uncommon for our employees. No one else has a problem with it. Well, by no one else I was referring not just to our current employee but former employees.

Employees of the past. I see. That's something that you will have to think about then. But not right now, on your own time, we're training right now.

Have you seen one of these before? That is correct. They're for the restrooms. If you need one of these tokens, just ask me or Miranda and we'll give you one. They're downstairs. We do not, under any circumstances, give these tokens to the customers. Tell customers that that may go to the Starbucks across the street. These tokens are strictly for the employees. No, just the employees. Because the managers use a separate restroom upstairs. You ask a lot of questions, don't you? It was my idea to install the lock on the restroom door and put these tokens to use. I felt that our employees were taking advantage of our rather lax break policies. I felt it would be best if employees didn't just disappear for minutes at a time and Miranda agreed with me. This way, we can limit the number of unnecessary breaks that are taken. I should also mention, before I forget, that cellular phones do not work in the employee restroom. You don't have a phone? Well, I guess it won't matter to you that there is no reception down there. Just keep that in mind if you do get one.

Cell phones don't work in there, nor are they permitted. We have a system of leadership here. The owner? His name is Henry but he doesn't come in very much because he lives in the Florida Keys with very bad arthritis, so it is up to us to keep things together. We do everything. We stock and do the ordering, we shelve the books, we run the totals at the end of the day. It's a lot to take in. Don't worry. Your application stated that you graduated magna cum laude? You'll catch on. You did well on the application. Most people think that when we ask, on the application, what your favourite colour is, that we want a straight-up response. You know, red. Or green. But we don't. We're looking for some creativity. You were playful with it. I noticed that.

You have probably noticed by now that we do not offer, as some of the other, larger bookstores do, chairs. We don't want to promote reading in the store. This is not a library. It is a place of business. We have too many people streaming through here on a day-to-day basis. There is an undeniable lack of room. Chairs would just cramp our space. Of course, in an ideal world, our customers would have pre-selected their book or books of choice before entering the premises. If our clients did their homework beforehand, that would be an enormous help to us. But as you will soon learn, that ideal customer is rare. People often want to sit down and browse through some of their selections. You see that we have several stools placed around the store. Those are actually for you, the employee, so that you can get up to the top shelves when you're shelving. No, it isn't dangerous. Just be careful. Well, because stools are less inviting than chairs. Because ladders are unwieldy. Because those "rolling things" as you refer to them are not high enough. Don't hesitate to ask a customer who is using a stool to give it back. We'll support you on that. On another note, you couldn't have known this unless you're a regular shopper here, which I know you're not since you just moved here. Anyway, I'm not chastising you, but employees are asked to wear black pants and black shirts. When you come in tomorrow, do you think you'd be able to do that? Nothing special, we don't demand that you wear a uniform or anything, but if you could just wear the black pants and shirt. That works best for us.

As for the pyramids, I'm not going to go into all the details today because it's a difficult task but basically, as you can see, some of the books are stacked in the form of a pyramid. This takes some skill, so you won't be able to get it on the first or second or even the third try. But keep working at it and eventually it will come. It's a bit like playing that game Jenga, except the stack is a pyramid instead of a box shape, for obvious reasons of customer convenience and product appeal. Have you played Jenga before? Well, you'll feel like you've played it once you start working on the pyramids. Oh, something I should have told you right away. I always forget. I know you like books, you said as much on your application. And we respect that, we really do. But when some people come to work here, some of them assume that since this is a bookstore, they'll have plenty of time to read books. Just so you know, that is not the case, and I thought I should mention it now so that there's no confusion later on. We have a very strict rule about that. Just keep in mind that there is always something that you can be doing. We have a preference for employees who prefer being busy. For example, if the books are properly stacked in the right pyramid formation, you can always go through the stock, which you'll learn about. There is always shelving to be done. If there is no shelving to be done, you could always re-organize the books into a cleaner pyramid. Should you do that and find that you have nothing left to do, a good thing we like to see is dusting. Of course it is very unlikely that you would ever be dusting, since it takes hours and hours to go through each and every book on the shelves to make sure that they are alphabetized correctly. Under no circumstances should you be caught reading. Should you be caught reading, that could unfortunately end in immediate termination.

I probably shouldn't say anything to you about this, but you seem very intelligent, and I just want to give you the heads up. The thing is that one of these days, a manager spot is going to open up. Miranda is very close to finishing her book. She's almost ready to send it out to Little, Brown, which is her publisher of choice. She's just deciding on a name really, plus doing some final rewrites. She expects it will just be a couple more months now, she is that close. Once she sends it out, I'm sure that things will change around here. We'll be very sorry to lose her; she is part of the glue that keeps this place together in many ways. But we'll go on, as they say. And when Miranda leaves, and I move up to head manager, we'll probably be looking for another manager. I shouldn't tell you this but you seem like a good listener and I thought your application was very clever. What was it that you wrote? Under favourite colour? It's a trick question but you got it right. Yes, that's it. The weary blues, the weary blues, the weary blues. Miranda and I caught the reference, of course. But what really stood out to me was that you wrote it three times like that. We thought that was very clever. So maybe one day you'll move up to manager, which is great because you'll automatically get the manager discount, even if you haven't been here for three months. It's a slightly larger discount than the employee discount, but I'm not at liberty to disclose the difference. As you can see, being a manager is a great job. Don't worry about it though, I know how complicated it seems, we don't expect you to have it all figured out on the first day. Everything is going to be fine. With my help, you'll sort it out, it won't take long.

*

AT LAST at SEA

"MY DEAR, YOU WILL love it," my mother had told me over the phone from Toronto, lingering on the L, attending to the V. "You'll just love it," she said again, as I wrapped the phone cord around my wrist like a bracelet, staring out at the palm tree in my backyard. "It's just glorious. I'll fly in and stay with you, and we'll board the ship from San Diego. You'll see."

But I don't like being in a place where the doors don't lead to land and each day begins and ends like the one before it. No newspapers, no cooking, no cash, and the only thing to see out the window is ocean. Grey, blue, white and water, water, water. It doesn't even seem that we're moving.

When the elevator reaches the lido deck, the door opens

on a gaggle of little kids in bathing suits. One of them, a small girl about five, is wearing orange flotation devices on her arms. I've seen her in the water every day, splashing around and giggling.

"Hi, Fishy," I say, and wave. We had a conversation in the pool yesterday. She explained to me, her eyes big and round and earnest, that she was a dolphin-in-a-whale-fishy-boat. My mother is already making her way toward the buffet. Fishy waves back.

*

Lounge chairs line the rim of the pool on the lido deck, employed mostly by ladies in old-fashioned bathing suits with oily, rubbery skin, many of whom have positioned sheets of aluminium under their faces to catch the sun. The majority of the ship's passengers appear to be these old ladies, travelling in twos and threes, though there is the occasional husband, plate heaped with food, lingering behind a more ambulatory wife. And there are some younger couples too, celebrating, I can only imagine, first and second anniversaries. I wish my mother had a group of friends to cruise with, to play mah-jong with, to talk to.

Across the deck at the buffet my mother is gesturing to me. She picks up a piece of something from a plate and pops it into her mouth. As she begins to chew, she stabs her finger three times towards the plate, and then at me, and then again at it. I recognize this pantomime. I shake my head no, and then she repeats the same series of gestures. The man beside her is staring. When she points at the food again, thrusting her finger towards it more forcefully, and for the third time, he goes around her.

She is wearing only a purple bathing suit and a straw hat, a pair of enormous sunglasses overwhelming her small face. I feel embarrassed, but in fact, I'm embarrassed to be embarrassed. This is my mother, with the good intentions, the incessant worry ("For your welfare, dear"), and the endless, inane stories of minor domestic disturbances (a raccoon-in-the-garbage-can might last up to half an hour, complete with a detailed denouement outlining the steps taken to protect the garbage against another attack). And she is also, at times, poetic, as when she wrote to me in an email about the mother of a bride: "That bitch Anne will be cool and elegant in some invisible little number, and I envision myself sweating, red-faced, and thirsty."

My mother is talking to a woman who is also wearing a straw hat, her hair pulled back into a neat bun. This woman is lean and well dressed, in linen pants and a blousy top. She is perfectly attired for a luxury cruise, though that is not quite what this is. I bob around in the pool for a while, my ears just below the surface.

*

Later, in our tiny room, my mother is sitting on the sofa smoking a cigarette. She tells me she's made a friend. "Another woman whose daughter hates her," she says. "It's interesting, we were talking about it, and this woman is a sociologist, but she says she doesn't know why her daughter hates her. She said it just happens that way sometimes, and there's nothing you can do about it."

"Maybe your friend the sociologist needs a therapist," I say.

"Maybe you do."

"I'm going back to the pool," I say, and walk out of our room, directly towards the casino.

*

Our first night on the ship we were placed at a dining table with six others: an elderly couple, neither of whom could hear very well, two sisters, both former schoolteachers, and two women named Cathy—friends in their mid-forties, both from San Diego, both blonde, both former bombshells.

The dining room was set elegantly, with white cloth draped over the tables, linen stuffed into the wine glasses, and chandeliers, at least seventy of them, above every table, dripping with glass that was not crystal but looked it.

"Well," my mother said, to no one in particular, and inhaled deeply, as if preparing to answer a question that hadn't yet been asked. Both Cathys looked at her.

"Isn't this nice?" she said, exhaling and unfolding a cloth napkin. The Cathys nodded.

"Is this your first time on a cruise?" one of the Cathys, the one with slightly shorter, blonder hair, asked.

"Oh no!" my mother said. "Oh no, no! I sailed to Peru last year. This is, in fact, my fourth cruise. And not my last!" She paused. "Unless I pop off suddenly!"

She looked at me and laughed a deep, miserable laugh. I noticed one of the schoolteachers, whose name I had already forgotten, eye her sharply. Oh, fuck off, I thought at the schoolteacher. Just you fuck off.

Our first course was served, a spinach salad with little chunks of canned, white asparagus, tomatoes, and bacon, and I began to pick at it, moving the bacon out of the way with my fork.

The same Cathy spoke up. "I've never been to Mexico before, except T.J. I mean *real* Mexico. But I'm so excited. I hope I can bring back some nice things. It's so cheap."

My mother seemed to have misunderstood Cathy to mean she was concerned about crossing the border with her new Mexican treasures because she proceeded to launch into an almost frantic explanation of the U.S. customs system, which, she said, was hardly any different from the Canadian one, and assured Cathy that border patrol was only looking for people who were attempting to transport serious drugs, firearms, or cash.

I watched the teacher as she wielded her knife and fork to cut the spinach into more manageable pieces and then halved the already small tomatoes and speared them onto her fork. She made little "Uh-huh" sounds and nodded, without looking, in my mother's direction.

By dessert, my mother was still talking—to no one in particular, it seemed—about *The Antiques Roadshow*, her mouth full of chocolate cake, and a small piece of asparagus clinging to the side of her chin. I had been staring at her for a long time, ready to point at that spot on my own face, but she never looked at me. The elderly couple had, by then, excused themselves, and the schoolteachers were talking quietly, almost whispering, to each other.

"So what are you going to do now?" I asked, as we were drinking our coffee.

"What the hell do you care?" she said, suddenly violent. "You're certainly not going to spend any time with me."

"You know," I said, "if you perhaps tried to ask people some fucking questions and then waited long enough to listen to their responses, you might actually make some fucking friends."

"My daughter with her beautiful language and her advice. Thank you, my darling. I will certainly keep that in mind the next time I'm at dinner with a bunch of sullen witches."

Our dinner companions pretended not to hear. Whatever symphony had been piped into the dining room had been turned off.

When I reach the casino I see the Cathys sitting at the bar. They smile at me as I near.

I'm not sure how to address them. "Hi, ladies," I say.

"Hi," the blonder Cathy says. "We haven't seen you guys at dinner lately."

"Oh," I lie. "We've been eating in our room."

"Your mom's a real riot," she says. The other Cathy smiles into her cocktail.

"Yep," I say. And then, because I can think of nothing else, no questions, I shrug and walk away. I have twenty bucks in my pocket, and I cash it into chips and sit down at the blackjack table. I bet it all on my first hand, which is a blackjack, and my subsequent hands are nearly all winners. Within a half hour I'm up $180. The croupier, Dave, is friendly, and what's more, he seems pleased that I'm winning. I feel better than drunk.

"Well," I say, savouring the sound the chips make as I stack and restack them with my thumb and forefinger, and thinking suddenly of an accordion. "I guess you gotta know when to fold 'em."

"OK, good," Dave says. "Good on ya."

"I know, huh?" I say, surprised by my own restraint.

*

When I return to our cabin, my mother is still sitting on the little blue sofa. The TV is tuned in to the ship's channel, a closed-circuit surveillance camera on the top deck; you can see the tip of the boat's bow, but mostly just what's in front of us. There's no land in sight.

Her face is hard set, her jaw clenched, her mouth a frown. She sweeps her eyes over me, from my face to my feet and back up again—a gesture I see teenage girls do a lot—and then she looks away, at the ashtray, her drink. Her eyes are red.

"You are," she says slowly, nodding her head a bit, "a very bad daughter." She says this as if it were the conclusion to a conversation that had been going on for a long time. And I suppose that, in many ways, it is.

"Uh-huh," I say, but what I really think is that we have a very small room and I wonder if Dave the croupier would like to fuck me and I wonder how late the ship's bars are open. "You have some spinach on your chin," I say, which isn't true.

*

I close the door behind me and walk down the tiny passageway, towards the elevator, thinking I'll go to one of the bars. A few doors down I see Fishy, still wearing her bathing suit, her orange flotation devices still attached to her arms.

"Hi, Fishy!" I say.

"No!" she says, shaking her blonde head, her damp hair flapping around her face. "No no no, I told you. I'm a whale-in-a-dolphin-in-a-fishy-boat!"

"Oh," I say, as if it was all clear to me now. "I understand. That's very interesting, though, because you know what?"

"What?"

"I'm a dolphin."

"No!" she says, unconvinced, her mouth open, shaking her head. "Nuh-uh."

"Yep," I say. "It's true. I am a dolphin. I'm a dolphin in a girl suit. That's why you can't tell right away."

Fishy looks me over carefully. At first I think she is about to laugh, but then her features twist and she wrinkles her nose and shuts her eyes, and when she opens them again they are brimming with salty little tears.

"No, Fishy," I say, alarmed. But she lets out a loud, terrified wail, all her teeth in view. "It's OK, it's OK, dolphins are nice."

But she is scared and I don't dare touch her. As she cries, she reaches up toward the handle of her cabin door, but she's too little and she fumbles with it, twisting it in the wrong direction. I hear footsteps and then the door opens, and Fishy is scooped up by her mother and then gone, the door locked quickly behind them. "Mommy!" I hear the girl cry, and I stand there, still as salt air, but I can't make out any words, just more crying, then her mother, who murmurs, and a few light sobs, and then, later, nothing.

*

REAL PEOPLES

IT'S BEEN THREE HOURS NOW on the Pacific Coast Highway and your legs are starting to cramp. When you stretch them you end up with one foot inside a plastic bag, which is only vaguely amusing because it is demoralizing. He's gripping the wheel of the rental, a cigarette dangling from his lips. Underneath his chin the skin is saggy, soft, and very white. You imagine what he would have looked like twenty years ago, at your age. He might still have had cheekbones and he probably wasn't fat yet. His career as a rock star was long over by then. He was already managing bands, trying to get a law degree on the side. He was going to be an entertainment lawyer. He sees you. What? He says it defensively. Pull over, you tell him. Pull over, I've got to pee. In a bit, he says.

The car smells fusty, like sour milk, sweat, smoke. It's

him. He didn't shower this morning, just got up out of bed and rummaged around on the floor for his things. He reminds you of a boyfriend you had once, but it was a long time ago, and the memory is fuzzy: you were probably twenty, still in Kingston, drunk most of the time. You can't even remember his name. It seems a shame.

*

You heard someone yelling outside the motel, C'mon, let's go, and you heard him, too, his creaking and moaning, his shit-fuck-fuck-me's. You poked your head out from under the covers and twisted your neck to watch him stuff himself into his expensive jeans and motorcycle boots, then run pomade through his hair, slicking it back and puffing it up at the front like a little pompadour. When his cell rang, he checked the caller ID and marched into the bathroom. You could hear him in there, too, his yes-no-right-I'll-call-him's. He came out of the bathroom and sat down next to you, messed with your hair. You could hear her voice on the other end, nothing like you thought it would sound, and you should know better, you should.

*

You have never been to California. The sun is bright; the light reflected through the car window is warm. The road weaves along the side of the mountain and in the distance you see a lighthouse, pastel blue and white. Now you see why he had insisted you take this road instead of the other one, the real freeway that you had wanted to see, a freeway you heard had six lanes on either side. The ocean stretches out beside you, twinkling.

*

I don't want to get in before the act does anyway, he'd said. They don't appreciate me and I sure as hell don't want to end up combing the city for the perfect fucking grilled cheese sandwich again. I'm not a runner, eh? But apart from his vitriol for the band he was in his Hollywood mood, optimistic and casual. He was going to charm you with his generosity, spread California out to you like a dessert tray, beam and nod with pride—unfounded, since it wasn't as if he lived here either. But that was before he realized how much time this route would tack on to the trip. Now, his knuckles are white, he's driving thirty miles an hour, and the signs on the road warn of falling rocks.

*

He paid the nine dollars and took you through the Seventeen Mile Drive and Pebble Beach and you rolled down the windows and gawked at the houses; big, modern marvels you couldn't even fathom living in, all of them facing the water. Who lives there, you wondered. What kind of life is that? The road is narrow and there is nowhere for a car to stop. You know this is deliberate, that these people don't want you to park and stroll all over their well-manicured beach. You saw a woman in the distance riding a horse along the shore, and as he clucked at the homes, reciting their likely values—thirty million, fifteen million, twenty—you stared at her, aware of a stupid jealousy taking root. What is the point, you ask yourself, but you want what you think she has. Everywhere, you are unwelcome.

*

You are relieved to get back on the old highway. To the east is sand and green, and in the distance, mountains. To the west, nothing but water. Great white rocks dot the landscape and lying on top of them are seals, lumbering and flopped out over them. But beyond that, you want to know, past the water and low clouds, what is beyond that?

Japan, he says. No, we're too low for Japan. Korea, maybe. We're at the ends of the earth, baby. He talks to you sometimes as if you are his accomplice or his friend, as if you were running away together. This is hardly the case. When you get to L.A., after the show, you'll fly home alone. Your little Oakville condo will look more depressing than ever, the Formica countertops and plywood furniture, the beige bathroom and ugly little tub. All of it will be there exactly as you left it, and you will wonder again and again and again if maybe there is something else you could do with your life. This is something you should have done in your twenties, when you might have been forgiven your stupidity, your selfishness.

*

As you drive, the mountains to the east edge in closer until you are hedged in by them on the one side and a cliff that plunges downhill for miles on the other. If he went too fast, or didn't take a turn well, you would both be dead. This would be worse for him than it would for you. He runs his fingers through his hair and swears again. It's going to take us another seven fucking hours at this rate. You haven't seen an exit sign or even a gas station in over an hour. Ahead of you, an old station wagon hobbles along and sets the pace. If this fucking car would get out of the way we could get moving, he says, but fuck me if I'm going to pass them on this road. You poke your baby finger through a hole in the vinyl seat and wish he would turn on the radio.

*

The night before in San Francisco, you met up with his friend—a former college football star who somehow ended up in the music industry. He met you both after the show in the motel bar. The place was full of German tourists and thin men wearing polyester shirts. They danced, some of them alone, some of them in small groups of three or four.

Let's get the hell out of here, the friend yelled. C'mon.

So you climbed into the friend's convertible and drove, the wind howling, and the friend drove fast, up hills and down. At a stoplight you turned around to face him. He looked oversized and out of place in the back seat. It made you feel sorry for him.

I'd like to live here, you said, but what you meant is that you have nothing much to give up at home. I could see you living here, he said. You asked him if he would visit you and he said maybe. Come on, you said. You looked at the people on the streets, hanging out in front of bars, talking, smoking. There were palm trees there. I'd like more money, he said, as if negotiating with you. I'd like to keep my mistresses in style.

The light turned green and the car lurched forward. The friend looked over at you and raised his voice. Your mistresses have enough style as it is, boy, he said, and took one of his enormous hands from the steering wheel and laid it on your thigh. You considered that you were not being treated with much dignity. Also, if he had more money, you are pretty sure he would not spend it on you.

The friend brought you to a bar and told you it was a famous jazz spot. You sat down on the plush velvet seat, put your elbows on the sticky tabletop, ordered scotch from the sleepy waitress who stood above you, one hand on her hip, a pen behind her ear. The band was gone. A drum kit sat at the back of the stage, the words "Lands Ends Trio" printed on the bass.

Fuck music, anyway, the friend said. Am I right? How was the show?

But he didn't wait for an answer. He drained the contents of his glass in one quaff and stood up to maneuver his huge body out of the booth. Be right back, he said, and you saw he had his phone in his hand. You sipped on the good scotch and tapped your finger against the table. Finally you said the word that had been bouncing around your brain: Mistress. Mistress? As if it were a word you did not understand.

*

He despises driving. Once, back home, he called you from the highway, two hours from where you were meeting. He told you he'd be late, and he sounded drunk and thwarted. He mumbled an apology and hung up. You bathed in the big tub and shaved your legs, ordered a burger from room service, and turned on the TV, falling asleep to the drone of some late night infomercial. He stumbled in eventually, and you were still asleep when he climbed into the bed next to you. You woke at dawn, his elbow tucked neatly under your trachea, the length of his forearm pressed firmly down onto your chest. You made as if to scream but didn't and instead you closed your eyes. He stopped. Shhh, he whispered, and stroked your hair. Shhh, real peoples, he said. Real peoples, okay? It is the nicest thing he's ever said to you.

*

When you see the Porsche behind you he is reaching for a cigarette from the pack on the dashboard. It comes into sight from a bend in the road and is behind you so quickly that you don't have time to say anything before it roars past you, a photograph with the aperture too low. It breaks into the wrong lane, and passes the station wagon in a blur. He has his foot on the brakes before you know it, but the station wagon veers sharply to the right and then skids into the shoulder towards the edge of the freeway. You close your eyes because you do not want to see what happens next: the station wagon simply dropping out of sight. You don't scream. It is a long drop. Everything is flatness. Everything is ugly, irrevocable.

You feel you are there in the middle of the road for a long time, so when you do open your eyes, and see that what you thought you saw did not in fact happen, you feel so removed it is as though the whole thing were unfolding in a movie on a screen at a drive-in. He is gripping the wheel beside you hard, staring straight ahead. You want to get out of the car and run over to those people but instead you take off your seat belt and whisper come on, we're in the middle of the road. He takes his foot off the brake and lets the car glide gently to the shoulder.

The car ahead of you has stopped inches from the cliff. I thought they were going to go over, he says, removing his seat belt and opening the door. I thought that was the end. You nod but he is already out of the car, walking towards the couple and the station wagon. Now you will definitely miss the show. And the police. They will have to be called.

You watch as the driver's door opens and a young man appears. You see him move around towards the other side of the car, where a young woman emerges, holding a small bundle in her arms. The man moves towards the woman, as if to embrace her, but she steps back and you can see she is shaking. The man carefully takes the bundle from the woman's arms and holds it to his chest, and the woman drops to the ground on her haunches. She wraps her arms over her head, her elbows sticking up in front of her. Below them the clouds meet up with the horizon, making a tidy line separating blue from white.

*

ACKNOWLEDGEMENTS

"We Could Be Like That Couple From That Movie That Was Playing Sometime" was published in *Headlight Anthology* and *Rising To A Tension* (Cumulus Press). "You Think It's Like This But Really It's Like This" was published in *Matrix Magazine*. "At Last At Sea" appeared in *THIS Magazine*.

Thanks to Malin Holmquist, Nikki Goldman, Jason Last, Ethan Wills, Helen Cretu, Rick Beauchemin, Ariel Smith, Jonathan McConnell, and Dylan Young. You are my friends and sometimes colleagues, and you are creative and inspiring.

Thanks to Paul Leonard, whose initial encouragement was integral.

Thanks to my publisher, Mike O'Connor, for his hard work and support.

Thanks to my editor, Jon Paul Fiorentino, for his patience, insight, humour, dedication to emerging writers, and his belief in me.

Special thanks to my terrific designer and dear friend, Gillian MacLeod. I'm nothing short of honoured that you agreed to take this project on. You saved the day.

Special thanks to Christopher Jacot and Matthew Finlason: my favourite team.

A huge debt of gratitude is owed to Steven Smith, Leah Finkel, and David McGimpsey, who read many of these stories over the years and generously offered their time, insight, and wit. I would especially like to thank Ryan Arnold for his continued support, his counsel, his invaluable criticism, and his ability to keep up the sound beats tiger.

Finally, an enormous thank you to Jayce Newton. My best friend, my love. Fig, I couldn't have done it without you.

*